GARY NORTHFIELD

CANDLEWICK PRESS

For my wonderful friend
and studio-mate, Sarah McIntyre

Special thanks as always to Lizzie and Jack, and to Lucy,
for their editorial and designer skillz and their deep reserves of patience

Copyright © 2016 by Gary Northfield

First U.S. edition 2018

Library of Congress Catalog Card Number pending
ISBN 978-0-7636-7854-8

17 18 19 20 21 22 BVG 10 9 8 7 6 5 4 3 2 1

Printed in Berryville, VA, U.S.A.

This book was typeset in Stempel Schneidler.

Candlewick Press
99 Dover Street
Somerville, Massachusetts 02144

visit us at www.candlewick.com

CONTENTS

So, you think you know about

JULIUS ZEBRA?

Well, you're probably

WRONG!

Julius wasn't quite like other zebras. Not only did he live during ROMAN TIMES, but he was also the

PEOPLE'S CHAMPION!

EXCITING, RIGHT?

❦ CHAPTER ONE ❧

THE PEOPLE'S CHAMPION

Walking through the noisy, smelly, bustling streets of Rome, Julius felt like Caesar himself! The place smelled worse than a gnu's backside, a lot like the stinky lake back home, but here, unlike back home, everybody LOVED him.

1

Since his triumphant, surprise victory at Rome's greatest amphitheater, the Colosseum, only a month ago, Julius had been transformed into a GLADIATOR SUPERSTAR!

Stories of his deeds had spread like wildfire throughout the vast empire. People were coming from all over just to see Julius fight, and he was loving every minute of it.

Scurrying next to Julius was his friend Cornelius the warthog. Cornelius was a rather small fellow, and in the melee of the crowded street, he had to fight hard not to be stepped on.

"Stop panicking, Cornelius!" said Julius as he waved merrily to his fans. "We have PLENTY of time. Let the people of Rome enjoy their hero walking among them!"

Cornelius tutted. "Careful—soon your head might get too big to walk down these narrow streets."

Just then, a scruffy young girl approached Julius, holding out a ratty parchment.

Julius ruffled the little girl's hair. "Of course, my dear little thing—do you have any ink?"

The girl looked very sad. "No . . ." She sighed.

Julius looked around the street to see what he could use to make a print. "How about if I dipped my hoof in mud? You'd have your very own Julius Zebra muddy hoofprint!"

The little girl's face lit up. "Oh, yes, please, Mr. Zebra. That would be wonderful! Thank you!"

Julius bent down and squished his front right hoof into the mud, then placed it very carefully onto the girl's parchment. He pulled his hoof away to reveal a perfect print.

"THAT IS SO AMAZING! THANK YOU, MR. ZEBRA!" squeaked the girl. "I LOVE YOU!" She kissed the print and ran off to a group of her friends standing nearby, who all squealed like little mice and jumped for joy at such an exciting souvenir.

Julius sniffed his hoof, screwing up his nostrils. "You know, I don't think that was actually mud."

He passed his hoof to Cornelius to sniff.

"Quick!" said Cornelius. "Let's go the other way. We'll be long gone before she notices." And they scooted off into the crowds.

"WAIT!" cried a voice. "WHERE ARE YOU GOING? WAIT FOR ME!" From one of the many shops that lined the street bounded a lively antelope clutching a lump of rock.

"Let me guess, Felix," said Julius. "Is it a rock?"

"Well," said Felix proudly, "what I have here is an actual piece of the PYRAMID OF GIZA IN EGYPT!"

Cornelius examined the rock carefully. "The only 'Giza' this rock has seen is the sneaky geezer who sold you this worthless junk!" he said with a huff. "These Roman shopkeepers see you coming a mile away, Felix. I don't know why you keep buying these stupid rocks."

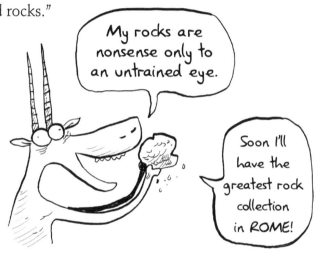

"Forget all that," said Julius. "Where are the others? We promised to meet them here at noon!"

"Yes!" agreed Cornelius. "As I keep saying, we need to head back to the Colosseum. Julius has an important fight this afternoon in front of the emperor to celebrate the Festival of Quinquatria!"

"The Festival of *Quinquatria*!" corrected Cornelius. "It is a festival to honor Minerva. She's the goddess of wisdom, so it's not surprising you've never heard of her."

"Well, that's RUDE!" snorted Felix.

Julius put his arms around his friends. "Stop it now, you two!" he said with a laugh. "Don't forget, Emperor Hadrian has finally PROMISED us our FREEDOM if I win this fight!"

"JULIUS!" cried a voice in the crowd. "JULIUS, WAIT!"

Julius turned around, expecting to greet one of his many fans, but was instead faced with the beaming sharp teeth of a smiling crocodile.

"LUCIA!" said Julius, pleased to see his friend. "How was the chariot racing?"

"A-MA-ZING!" she said.

The Greens won again!

We smashed the rotten Blues right off the track.

"Rufus found you a present, too!" she squealed.

"He did?" asked Julius excitedly, clapping his hooves. A long shadow loomed over Julius, who looked up to see his friend Rufus the giraffe.

"I did!" replied Rufus, and he handed a tiny statuette to the eager zebra.

"Look! It's a figurine of YOU!" said Lucia.

"That's AWESOME!" exclaimed Felix. "It even has your crazy bug-eyes!"

Julius fired a dirty look toward Felix. "WHAT crazy bug-eyes?"

Rufus interjected, "They had a big stall selling hundreds of them! You are REALLY famous now!"

As if on cue, an excited mob started to crowd around the animals to see the gladiator superstar walking down their street.

"Come on!" said Cornelius. "We really should head back before this bunch tears us apart."

The animal friends pushed through the frenzied crowd onto the main road that ran through the heart of Rome. Dashing under the arches of the great aqueduct and past the grand palace that sat up on the hill, they headed for the huge stone stadium looming large on the horizon.

They raced past the crowd massing around the Colosseum and then dashed right PAST the Colosseum.

Instead, they ran into an unassuming square building next to the amphitheater, past the gruff guards at the door, and into a huge courtyard that housed its own mini-arena.

This was Ludus Magnus, Rome's biggest and best gladiator school and home to Julius and his pals. The *click-clack* of wooden swords could be heard as gladiators honed their fighting skills, but there was no time to stand and watch. They raced downstairs toward the tunnel that led directly to the underbelly of the Colosseum, only to find their way blocked by a scrawny, surly lion.

"Sorry, Milus!" gasped Julius, catching his breath. "But we had a terrible time trying to outrun my hordes of fans!"

Milus just tutted and stepped to one side. "You have a hard life, Zebra," he growled sarcastically. "Anyway, it's not me you've got to apologize to. It's PLINY!"

Julius slapped his forehead with his hoof. "Oh, no! I promised Pliny I'd meet him early to brush up on those new sword moves he's been teaching me."

He sprinted down the tunnel, the stench of the rancid dungeons hitting his nose as he ran. He careered around a corner, past the cages with the growling leopards, and toward one of the many lifts that brought the animals up into the arena.

The little mouse threw a gold helmet at Julius.

"You'd better get yourself suited and booted!" he said. "If you're ever gonna make a good impression in front of Hadrian, then today has to be the day!"

"Aw, you don't need no extra training!" Pliny laughed. "Your opponent is as useless as ALL the other animals you've had to face." The little mouse gave Julius a friendly punch on his shin. "There ain't no animal gladiator like YOU, Julianne!"

"It's JULIUS, not Julianne!" said Julius, rolling his eyes. "How many times do I have to tell you?"

"Julius, Julianne, Julio! Whatever!" replied Pliny, pushing Julius into his cage.

CHAPTER TWO
ZEBRAMANIA!

Julius's heart pounded as the cage lifted up toward the ceiling, scraping roughly against the stone walls. Over the creaking of the stiff wooden frames, Julius could clearly make out the chanting of the crowd. "ZEBRA! ZEBRA! ZEBRA!"

The cage stopped moving with a great THUMP, and Julius grabbed the wooden bars to keep himself from falling over.

Just above him he could hear the voice of the *summa rudis,* the referee.

"CITIZENS OF ROME!" bellowed the *summa rudis.* "As you all know, to celebrate the Festival of Quinquatria, Emperor Hadrian has decreed that you should enjoy a day of FEASTING and FIGHTING!" The crowd roared. "THE FIRST OPPONENT," he screamed, "Rome's very own PEOPLE'S CHAMPION, JULIUS ZEBRA!"

A trapdoor opened in front of Julius to thunderous cheers and the blast of a hundred trumpets. He bounded through the hatchway.

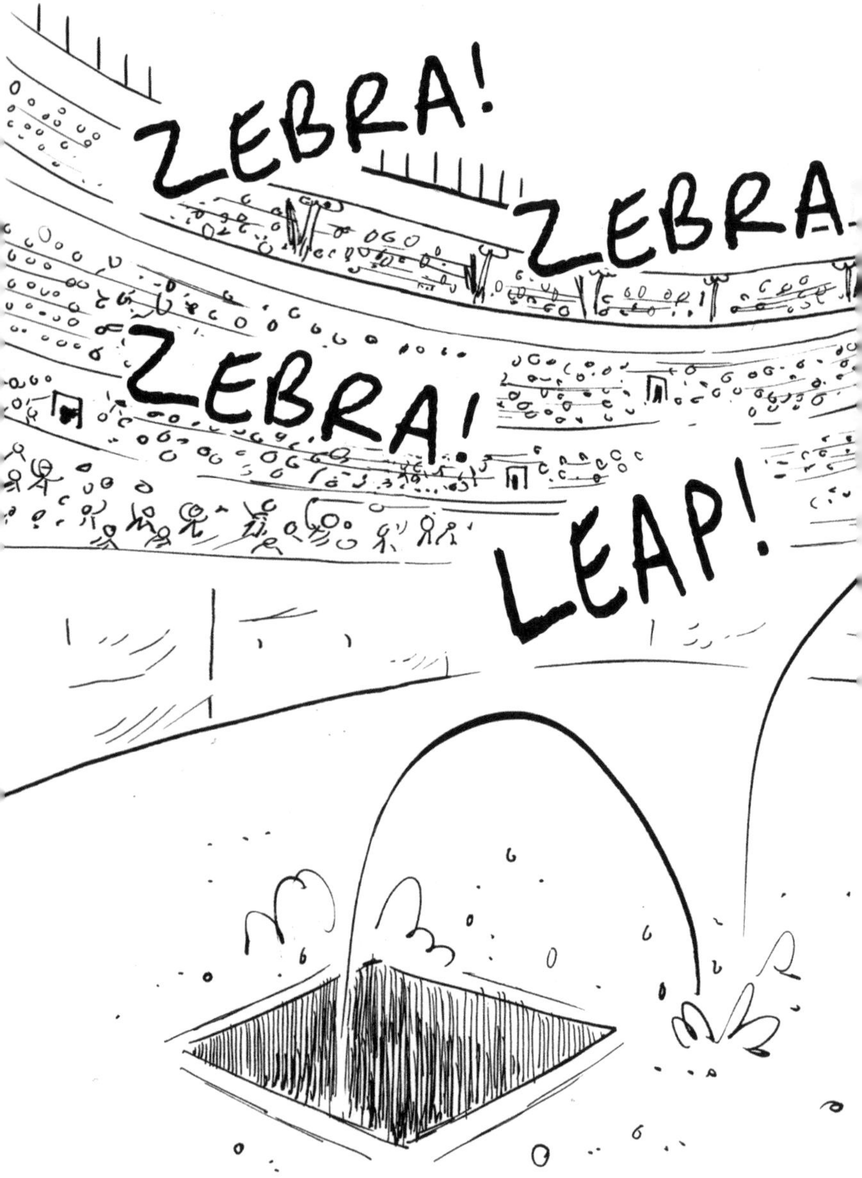

ZEBRA!
ZEBRA
ZEBRA!
LEAP!

Julius threw up his arms to greet the crowd of eighty-thousand roaring his name so loudly that the whole amphitheater shook.

Eager to show off his skills, Julius leaped into a backward somersault, throwing his sword into the air. Then he deftly caught it while landing nimbly on the arena floor like a cat. The audience erupted into another round of chanting and cheering.

Watching from the sidelines, Julius's friends were on their feet, clapping and cheering him along.

Over on the other side of the arena, in his gold-and-marble royal box, sat the Emperor Hadrian, enthusiastically applauding his zebra champion.

Excellent! thought Julius. *Hadrian seems to be in a good mood. There's no way he won't grant me my freedom today!*

In the center of the arena stood the *summa rudis,* a beefy man in a white tunic with two long blue parallel stripes. In his right hand, he held a big stick.

The *summa rudis* shouted to be heard.

"THE SECOND OPPONENT!" he screamed. "ALL THE WAY FROM THE CITY OF ALEXANDRIA, IN EGYPT, the mighty camel warrior IMHOTEP!"

From the gates, a camel came stumbling in, his loose, ill-fitting armor rattling as he scrambled across the arena floor. As he reached the *summa rudis,* he tripped over his spear and landed in a clattering heap on the floor.

The crowd roared with laughter.

On the sidelines, Milus shook his head in despair. "Where do they find these idiots?"

Julius took up his position in the arena and smacked his sword into his shield with a dramatic growl. This sent the crowd into another frenzy. Imhotep gulped and took a small step backward. He glanced over his shoulder as the zebra-crazy spectators hurled insults and rotten food in his direction.

Holding up their G-shaped horns, the *cornicines* trumpeted the start of the fight, and the *summa rudis* stepped aside. The Colosseum roared.

Flicking his sword from behind his shield, Julius edged confidently toward the twitchy Egyptian camel.

"GET HIM!" yelled the crowd. "LOP HIS HEAD OFF! FINISH HIM!"

Imhotep timidly shuffled backward, his armor jangling as he shivered with fear. "Come on!" cried Julius. "At least TRY to hit me with your spear. Give these guys a bit of a show. I promise I won't hurt

you too much!" The camel shook his head. Rotten
vegetables spattered his nice shiny headdress.

Imhotep finally collapsed onto the ground,
sobbing. "PLEASE DON'T KILL ME, ZEBRA!"
he cried. "DON'T BLOW ME UP WITH MAGIC
LIGHTNING FROM YOUR EYES!"

Julius stood over the blubbering camel and kicked his spear away with his hoof. "I shall spare your life, Imhotep," he declared. "No lightning shall pass from my eyes today."

"Come on," said Julius, turning to the crowd. "You think I should bust this camel's HUMP?"

Pliny turned to Milus. "Please tell me he didn't really just say that."

"I'm afraid he did," replied Milus flatly.

In the arena, the *summa rudis* grabbed Julius's arm and thrust it into the air. "THE WINNER!" he announced.

Julius turned to the royal box to seek the emperor's approval and his long-awaited promise of freedom.

But the royal box was empty. Hadrian was gone!

Julius's friends came dashing across the arena.

"Milus saw him get a message, then he stormed away in a huff!"

Julius flopped to the ground in despair. "But he PROMISED!" he wailed.

Felix tried to console him. "If it helps, Hadrian didn't look happy to leave. He was really enjoying himself until he bailed. . . ."

Julius looked like he was ready to burst into tears. "We'll NEVER win our freedom!" he whimpered. "We'll be stuck in this Roman dump for the REST OF OUR LIVES!"

As Julius dragged himself up and began to shuffle out of the arena, a familiar figure stood in his way. "Then you'll be pleased to hear my news, Donkey!" came a gruff voice.

"Septimus," groaned Julius.

The towering figure of the *lanista,* boss of the gladiator school, stood in front of them, hands on his hips.

Hadrian wants to see you in the morning.

Seems he has "exciting" news for you.

"OOH! A SURPRISE!" squealed Julius, clapping his hooves. "I LOVE surprises!"

"He wants to see you all in the school arena at sunrise," growled Septimus. "And make sure your knapsacks are packed. You're going on a nice long trip!"

Julius and the others were beside themselves with glee. "A LONG TRIP?" cried Julius. "WE'RE GOING ON VACATION!"

"I wouldn't trust these scoundrels as far as I could throw them," Milus growled. "The only trip we're going on is to the forests of Germania to face the BARBARIAN HORDE!"

CHAPTER THREE

ROMAN HOLIDAY!

At the first crow of the rooster the next morning, Julius sprang out of bed.

All the animals quickly got dressed, ate their bowls of oatmeal, and dashed down to the small arena in the center of the school.

Septimus strode in, clapping his hands. "LINE UP IN THE MIDDLE, YOU LOWLIFES! QUICKLY! QUICKLY!"

"BY THE FIERY BEARD OF JUPITER, WHAT DO YOU THINK YOU ARE ALL DOING?" Septimus bellowed. "I said pack your knapsacks, not dress up as CLOWNS!" He stormed up to Rufus, snatched his fishing rod from his hoof, and snapped it in two over his own knee.

"I ought to send you all straight to the galleys as punishment!" he yelled.

Septimus leaned in to Cornelius's face. "It's not FUN, Warthog, it's HORRIBLE!"

"Forget that!" cried Felix. "Tell us about this great vacation! Will there be pebble beaches?"

Milus grabbed Septimus by his tunic and pulled him up to his big teeth. "And please," he snarled, "be sure to explain how it is we're being sent on vacation, as opposed to being *set free . . . ?"*

Suddenly, from the east entrance to the arena, Emperor Hadrian strode in, flanked by elite Roman guards.

Milus reluctantly dropped Septimus, who harrumphed and adjusted his crumpled tunic.

Hadrian addressed the animals. "Listen to me, beasts: Julius's battle yesterday at the Festival of Quinquatria convinced me that he is one of the greatest champions of Rome." He walked up and down, looking at the animals proudly. "In fact, throughout the empire, you are now ALL legends, heroes that every man and creature aspires to be!"

Hadrian stopped in front of Julius and placed his hand on the zebra's shoulder. "So much so that I need you, my People's Champions, to go to the distant corner of our empire and INSPIRE my citizens!" He waved his fist triumphantly in the air. "I want you to show them what it means to be a WARRIOR ROMAN!"

I have arranged a tournament for you all.

Win that, and THEN I shall grant you your freedom!

He stared Julius right in his eyes. Julius blinked nervously.

"Sounds fair enough," he mumbled. "Where are we going, then? Gaul? Egypt? Will I need my sand toys?"

"We are sending you to BRITANNIA!" declared Hadrian. All the animals looked at one another, bewildered.

"BRITANNIA?" cried Julius. "Oh, how PERFECT!"

"Ah." Hadrian smiled, impressed. "You have heard of our exotic little outpost, then?"

"Ooh, no, never heard of it!" replied Julius. "I'm just excited about going on vacay!"

Cornelius's grin turned into a grimace. "I've heard of it," he whispered to Julius, "and it's not good."

Milus was also unconvinced. "So, we just turn up, entertain the locals, and then we can go free?"

"Yes!" replied Hadrian. "Something like that."

He turned to Septimus. "Get them ready, Septimus. The ship leaves at noon."

"YOU HEARD THE EMPEROR!" Septimus bellowed. "NOW PACK YOUR BAGS LIKE REAL WARRIORS AND BE READY AT NOON!"

Felix put up his hoof. Septimus nearly collapsed in frustration. "WHAT IS IT NOW?"

"Um, so *will* we be needing sand toys on this trip? Hadrian wasn't very clear."

What do YOU think?

Felix thought for a moment. "I'm thinking . . . yes?"

Septimus moved his head closer to Felix's face and let out a low growl.

"NO!" squealed Felix. "I mean, no!"

Septimus leaned back. "CORRECT answer! Now, get moving. And if I see one single sand toy, you'll ALL be on a one-way trip to the battlefields of GERMANIA!"

CHAPTER FOUR

ALL ABOARD!

By noon, everyone was packed and ready to leave. They jumped onto the back of a cart waiting to take them to the port of Ostia.

Julius was so excited that he decided it was time for a sing-along to get everyone in the vacation mood.

"Come on, everybody, after me! OH, I DO LIKE TO BE BESIDE THE SEASIDE!"

As the others joined in, Julius noticed that Septimus was having a quiet chat with his champion gladiator, Victorius.

"Those two are ALWAYS whispering to each other!" replied Cornelius. "They're like a couple of old busybodies."

Milus let out a big huff. "Well, I don't like it one bit. In fact," he growled, "I don't like this 'trip' one bit!"

Julius gave the lion a big ruffle of his ratty mane.

"You ALWAYS see the worst in everything! I'm just desperate to get this trip started!"

Julius leaned out of the cart and called out to Septimus. "COME ON! I'm sure you'll see each other again! Just give that idiot a big kiss and LET'S GET GOING!"

"ALL RIGHT, ALL RIGHT!" growled Septimus as he stormed to the cart and hopped onto his seat. "Insolent animals! If I had my way, you'd be well on your way to—"

And so, finally, they all sped off to the great Roman port of Ostia, where, an hour later, they found their ship waiting for them at the dock.

They ran onto the deck and began exploring the impressive vessel and all its nooks and crannies.

"Right, you dopes!" shouted Septimus as he came on board. "Line up on the deck NOW!" They all scooted to the middle of the ship, lining up as instructed. Septimus marched up and down, looking at them sternly. "This voyage is going to be a VERY LONG one, and I intend to keep you all busy on this ship."

Do you mean doing jumping jacks?

"CORRECT!" cried Septimus. "I DO mean doing jumping jacks. AND peeling potatoes and any other awful jobs I can think of to keep you out of trouble!"

"BAH!" blurted Milus. "I told you! Some vacation this is going to be!"

Ignoring the lion, Septimus continued with his lecture. "In fact, we will start with SCRUBBING this filthy deck! Everyone grab a bucket and brush. QUICKLY! I want it so clean and shiny I can see my FACE in it!"

As they all furiously scrubbed away, the ship pulled out of Ostia.

Farewell, old friend!

Julius polished the rotten wooden deck as hard as he could, but he was nowhere near getting anything like a shine on it. "This is pointless!" he gasped. "My arms will fall off before we see Septimus's ugly mug on this deck!"

Felix leaned over to Julius. "Milus was right: this isn't a vacation! This is WORK!" he whispered. "I think I would rather have stayed at gladiator school!"

Cornelius shuffled over to join in the grumbling.

Lucia and Rufus inched over to see what everyone was whispering about.

"Are you all moaning about doing these dumb chores?" asked Lucia very quietly, peering over her shoulder to make sure Septimus wasn't looking.

"Yeah, you could say that!" huffed Julius, struggling to keep his voice down.

Felix plopped his brush into the bucket of soapy water and straightened his stiff back. "I'm pretty sure vacation means going away and having a nice time," he whispered. "And I can tell you now, I am definitely NOT having a nice time —"

"In fact," roared Septimus, "you can all give me fifty jumping jacks!"

"WHAT?" blurted Felix, getting up on his hooves. "Did your mom take you on vacation to boot camp or something? This is RIDICULOUS!"

"Yes she DID, actually," replied Septimus, smiling fondly. "Best days of my life." He thumped Felix on the shoulder. "YOU can give me an extra fifty jumping jacks for being a wise guy." Then he disappeared toward his cabin.

Finally they all flopped to the floor, exhausted. "All I can say," wheezed Julius, "is that this tournament had better be worth it!"

"Fear not, Julius," Cornelius announced. "I have seen a sign that our fortunes are favored by the gods!"

Julius rolled his eyes. *Here we go again!* he thought. *Cornelius and his la-la superstitions.*

The warthog pointed to the big sail fluttering above them.

Cornelius then pointed to Felix, who had accidentally kicked over his bucket of water. "And see how water has been spilled? To spill water when the wind blows in from the east is a sure sign that Neptune, god of the sea, wishes us well on our voyage!"

"And a sure sign that Felix is a clumsy half-wit," growled Milus.

Suddenly, Septimus reappeared on deck.

"UH-OH! Watch out!" said Julius. "Look busy!"

Septimus paced up and down, scrutinizing the sparkling deck.

"Well?" Julius called out. "How did we do? Can you see your glorious face now?"

Septimus spun around and glared at the cheeky zebra. "All I see, Donkey, is a bunch of USELESS DEADBEATS!"

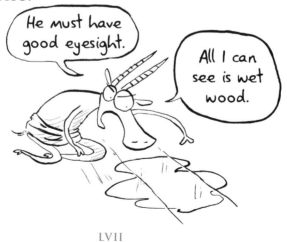

Septimus marched over to the exhausted animals. "You'll have to do better than this tomorrow, beasts. The empire won't tolerate a filthy ship."

From a knapsack he tossed small brown biscuits at the animals.

"Here's your dinner. Take these biscuits down to the hold, where you'll find your sleeping quarters. I'll see you back on deck AT THE CRACK OF DAWN." And he marched back to his cozy cabin.

Julius and his companions wearily pulled themselves up and headed toward the wooden ladder that led below deck, trailing stale biscuit crumbs behind them.

❦CHAPTER FIVE❦
STINK HOLE

As they clambered down the slippery ladder, they found a gloomy, very stinky hold. Julius jumped down the last few steps, only to splash into a big puddle.

EURGH!
This place is
soaked!

He squinted into the murkiness and could just make out piles of broken jugs and rotted crates from voyages past. As he edged forward, his face was suddenly tangled up in what felt like a huge cobweb.

The others came rushing over to rescue their stricken friend. "Don't panic, Julius!" called Cornelius. "We'll save you!" But the more they tried to pull Julius free, the more everyone got twisted up in the web.

From behind them came a low, growly laugh.

"A hammock? What's that?" asked Julius.

"What does it look like?" said Milus, lounging back comfortably. "It's a BED!"

"A BED?" cried Julius, befuddled. "How EXCITING!" He pulled the net off his friends and smoothed it out with his hooves. "Anything's got to be better than those rotten sleeping cells back in Rome!" He laughed as he leaped into the air, expecting to flop onto his strange new bed. But instead he fell right through the threadbare net and straight into the big puddle on the floor.

As he pulled himself up and wiped muddy water off his bottom, Julius let out a big sigh. "I'm not sure I can put up with these traveling conditions."

Cornelius tentatively pulled himself up onto a hammock, which seemed to hold his weight as it swayed with the rocking ship. "Hadrian thinks we're all People's Champions, but I think we're being treated pretty badly, don't you?"

"I tried to warn you!" said Milus. "These Romans are rotten to the core!"

"But what should we do?" asked Julius. "We're the PEOPLE'S CHAMPIONS! We should not be scrubbing floors!"

Lucia suddenly put up her claw. "Do not fear, my friends," she whispered, beckoning them to come closer.

She signaled to Rufus to check whether any Romans were listening from above. The giraffe poked his head up, then gave the all clear. The crocodile gathered everyone into a huddle.

"Before you start," interrupted Cornelius, "just so you know, I'm NOT wearing a stupid mustache." He scratched his nose.

I'm still itching after your last escape plan!

Scratch! Scratch!

"There'll be no mustaches—I promise," replied Lucia.

"But we *will* be wearing brightly colored checked pants again, right?" asked Felix. "I thought I looked PRETTY spiffy in those fancy pants last time."

Lucia shook her head. "Sorry, Felix, no fancy pants, either."

Felix let out a big HUFF and kicked a clay pot.

"This is DEFINITELY the worst vacation I've ever been on!" He sprang grumpily into his hammock, which flipped him over and dumped him onto the floor.

"What's the plan then, Lucia?" whispered Julius, rubbing his hooves together with anticipation. "Spill the beans!"

"Check this out!" she said, and from her knapsack she pulled out some very fine chain mail. "Rufus and I were poking around down here, and we found a whole stash of this stuff!"

"Enough? Enough for what?" asked Cornelius suspiciously. "Are we dressing up as soldiers and FIGHTING our way off the ship?"

"Nope!" said Lucia as she began wrapping herself in the chain mail.

"FISH?" everyone echoed in unison.

"Yes!" replied Lucia proudly. "This might not look like much at the moment—"

"You can say THAT again," growled Milus.

"BUT," she continued, ignoring the lion, "once Rufus and I have finished making the costumes, we'll all dress up as FISH, sneak up on deck, and JUMP into the sea!"

Cornelius was not impressed. "This has to be the most RIDICULOUS idea I've *EVER* heard!" He tugged at Lucia's chain mail. "As soon as Septimus or one of the other Romans hears a big splash, they'll look overboard and see us fools swimming around."

"EXACTLY!" chimed in Rufus. "But they won't see *US*. . . . They'll see FISH!" He held out his hooves as if he'd just performed the most amazing magic trick.

Lucia looked at the blank faces around the room. "And then we swim away and get FREE!" she added enthusiastically. "Don't you *see*? The chain mail looks like shiny fish scales! It's an AWESOME plan!"

Julius jumped up and had a good look at the chain mail for himself.

Hmmm...

You know what? I actually think this could work.

"It IS pretty shiny and slippery, just like fish scales," he said, holding it up to the light. "Maybe it's worth a shot!" He turned to the others. "Come on! Do you want to be scrubbing moldy decks and doing jumping jacks all the way to Britannia?"

Everyone shook their heads.

"NO. I just wanted a nice vacation like they promised," wailed Felix.

"OK, I'll do it," said Felix. "But only if I can be a halibut."

Julius patted him on his shoulder. "You can be whatever fish you want."

Felix jumped up and punched the air with his hoof. "Then I'm IN!" he roared.

Julius turned to Cornelius. "And you?"

"I'm coming, too!" said Milus. "It's a stupid plan, but I'm not hanging around on this lousy ship."

"Then it's decided!" declared Julius. "We'll help Lucia and Rufus make the costumes, and we'll make our escape as soon as the sun rises!"

CHAPTER SIX

GONE FISHING

"WAKE UP, YOU DEADBEATS!"
Septimus's voice boomed down the hatch. "TIME
TO GET UP AND SCRUB THOSE DECKS!"

Julius rubbed his tired, bleary eyes with his hooves.
They'd been up all night making fish costumes, and
now they had to put their plan into action.

Wakey wakey, everyone. Time to get this show on the road.

"We're going to need a distraction," said Julius. "I'll go up on deck and pretend to scrub. I'll keep Septimus chatting while you all jump in the sea."

"But what about you?" asked Cornelius. "Aren't you coming with us?"

"As soon as Septimus and the crew go to look at all you 'fishes,' I'll throw this on, then dive in after you," said Julius. "OK!" He bundled his fish costume into the bucket. "Are we all ready?"

"Don't forget," said Julius as he climbed the ladder, "wait till I've got Septimus talking before you jump overboard!"

He scampered up the ladder and out onto the deck, whistling innocently. He waltzed over to the far end of the boat and started pretending to scrub the deck.

Septimus stormed over to him. "WHAT'S GOING ON, DONKEY? WHERE ARE THE REST OF THE LAZY BEASTS?"

"That's our cue, lads!" whispered Lucia, and they sneaked up the ladder and out onto the deck.

Julius kept Septimus talking to distract him.

Septimus looked furious. "What are you babbling about, Donkey? I have no time for this nonsense!"

Behind Septimus there was a sudden shrill scream.

"WHAT IN JUPITER'S BEARD . . . ?" roared Septimus. He dashed to the side of the ship and saw a strange mass of figures thrashing about in the water.

"MAN OVERBOARD!" came the cry from the helmsman.

Septimus leaned over for a closer look. "Those *aren't* men! THAT'S A CROCODILE, A WARTHOG, A GIRAFFE, A LION, AND AN ANTELOPE!"

Having hastily put on his fish disguise, Julius flip-flapped to the side of the boat. "Wait! Surely they're FISH!" he cried. "See their shiny scales? Is that . . . a GIANT HALIBUT? Best let them go, Septimus!"

Septimus leaned over to get an even better look. "FISH? You are more of an imbecile than I gave you credit for, Donkey!"

Julius shrugged. "Oh, well. I tried!" And with that, he plunged into the sea with his friends.

Unfortunately, as soon as he plopped in, Julius realized that he could barely move.

In fact, the chain mail was dragging him under.

He frantically looked around and saw that all his friends were also struggling to stay afloat. "HELP US, SEPTIMUS!" cried Julius. "WE'RE DROWNING!"

Using boat hooks and a fishing net, the crew hauled the animals back on board with a big wet PLOP. They flapped about on the deck like floundering fish, but they weren't fooling anyone.

"SEND THESE BLUBBER BRAINS DOWN TO THE HOLD!" shrieked Septimus. "I'LL DEAL WITH THEM LATER!"

"I'm so sorry. I nearly killed us all off," sniveled Lucia as they were led down the hatchway. "I'll think of a better plan next time, I promise!"

"Don't worry about it," said Julius as he pulled off his costume. "It looks like we're going to have to stick it out on this stinking slave ship. Once we reach Britannia, we'll just need to make sure we win Hadrian's tournament—and our freedom."

"You really do live in a dream world, Zebra!" said Milus as he jumped into his hammock. "Hasn't this trip taught you ANYTHING about these Roman scoundrels?" He picked up his knapsack and started to rummage inside it. "The only escape from these wretches is DEATH!"

"Oh, nice!" said Julius.

Milus suddenly became very agitated and sprang out of his hammock.

He turned to Julius. "It must have been YOU!" he snarled. "While we were all splashing around in the water, you must have sneaked back here and eaten them!"

"Are you CRAZY?" said Julius. "I was distracting Septimus all that time!"

Milus hurled his knapsack to the floor and grabbed Julius by the throat. "Being stuck on a ship heading toward certain death with you NINCOMPOOPS is bad enough," he snarled, "but someone stealing my BISCUITS is the last straw."

CHAPTER SEVEN
LAND OF HOPE AND GORY

"Three weeks we've been stuck on this rancid ship. . . ." gasped an exhausted Julius, his head hanging over the side. "If I never see another wave again, it will be too soon."

"At least this time we haven't been cramped up in a tiny box," squeaked Cornelius, also hanging his green face over the side of the ship.

Julius let out a deep sigh. "Not only has Septimus got us working day and night, but I've got that INSANE LION thinking I yoinked his biscuits. Things couldn't be more unbearable!"

Cornelius looked up to the giant square sail, buffeting in the breeze. "Don't worry, Julius. We've had two days of fair wind, so we should be there very soon."

Julius gazed off into the distance. "I don't think I could suffEEUURGH!" He retched over the side again. "Sorry. . . . What I meant to say is, I don't think that I could suffer another day of this trip, Cornelius."

And where has your god Neptune been all this time?

Well, you're still alive, aren't you?

Cornelius plopped himself down on the deck, exhausted. "That Hadrian really is a jerk," he said. "He must have known what a long, treacherous journey this was going to be. I'll never forgive him for pretending it was some nice day out."

"Don't you worry, Cornelius," said Julius as he plonked down next to his friend. "Once we win the tournament, we'll show those Romans who they're dealing with!"

I'm the PEOPLE'S CHAMPION!

"HEY! WILL YOU TWO DIMWITS GET BELOW DECK?" boomed a voice from the captain's cabin. "UNLESS OF COURSE YOU ACTUALLY WANT TO BE WASHED OVERBOARD!"

The two seasick animals dragged themselves up and walked slowly back to the hatchway to the lower deck. But as they started climbing down the ladder, a great roar of "LAND HO!" came from the lookout on the bow of the ship.

They both turned to look. On the far distant horizon, a dark sliver of land began to appear through the mist.

All the other animals rushed up on deck and gaped at the strange new land.

"Exciting, but perhaps *very dangerous,*" warned Cornelius. "From what I understand, the local barbarians are extremely fierce and are none too happy about the Romans taking over their land."

"Yeah!" said Rufus nervously. "I heard some of the crew say that the place is swarming with gruesome monsters, like HEADLESS MEN!"

"Er, I'm not sure about the headless men," said Cornelius, "but there are *definitely* plenty of weird people living on this island."

Lucia became very excited. "Ooh, what fun! Like who? Who lives here?"

Well, I'm glad you asked!

Excited to be spouting facts

"The local inhabitants are called BRITONS.

They are a VERY tall
race and they walk in a
GOOFY WAY.

They like to roam around NAKED
in swamps all day.

They paint their bodies in amazing **INTRICATE PICTURES,** sometimes of animals, to harness their powers.

They are also **VERY FIERCE** because it is so cold and miserable. And when they get cold, they wear the SKINS OF ANIMALS!"

"You know what?" said Felix. "If I were to wear any one of you as a skin, it would probably be Julius. You'd make a lovely pair of stripey pants!"

"Thanks, Felix," said Julius. "Your antlers would also make a lovely hat."

"You leave my antlers out of this!" squealed Felix, putting his hooves up to defend them.

"I think I'm starting to look forward to this tournament!" said Julius. "I wonder what weird local animals we might be up against. I'm guessing they don't have camels or lions in Britannia."

"The only thing I'm looking forward to," growled Milus, "is finding out who ate my BISCUITS!"

"Oh, will you shut up about your STUPID biscuits?" muttered Julius.

CHAPTER EIGHT
BRITON ROCK

XCV

Julius and the other animals stood shivering on the deck as the ship drifted through the frozen mist. The gray-brown landscape with its scattering of skeletal trees loomed silently as they pulled into the dock.

Julius could make out what looked like a long wooden wall with a tower constructed at either end.

Wow! This is a million miles away from the crazy world of Rome.

As they thumped into the jetty, Julius spotted the unmistakable figures of Roman legionnaires standing atop the towers and along the wall, keeping watch over the comings and goings of the small port.

"That must be a fort," said Cornelius. "The Romans sure have a lot of troublemakers keeping them busy."

"Look at him all dressed up in his warm furs!" said Julius.

"It gets a BIT CHILLY up here," Septimus called out as he breezed past the trembling animals. "You might want to get yourselves wrapped up!"

"You know, Milus," sighed Julius, "I'm so glad your cheery, furry little face is always around to fill me with the joys of spring."

"COME ON! CHOP, CHOP! Don't just stand there!" barked Septimus. "Get your packs and follow me."

They grabbed their belongings from the hold and were led up the jetty to a waiting horse-drawn cart.

"Jump on the back. We're heading straight to Londinium, and we need to get there before dark. SO NO MESSING AROUND!"

Septimus marched off to fix the reins of the horses, and Julius looked over to the beach. "Say what you want about Britannia, but that really *is* a lovely beach."

"Just look at all those tide pools," said Rufus. "I bet you could find some crabs in there."

"Ooh!" cried Felix. "I bet there are some AWESOME rocks, too!" He dashed over to the water's edge and rifled through the pebbles and stones that lay scattered in the mud.

Meanwhile, Lucia and Rufus were wading in a big tide pool with a fishing net, trying to find something to catch.

"THERE!" cried Rufus. "A little crab! Get the little guy! Get him!"

I got him!
I got him!

Splash!

Cornelius, wearing his sun hat, joined Julius on the beach.

"Nice hat, Cornelius," said Julius.

"Why, thank you," said Cornelius, giving it a slight adjustment. "I know it's cold, but this hat makes me feel like I'm on vacation."

Suddenly, Septimus appeared, looming over them. "HAVE YOU ALL GONE INSANE?" he screamed, pulling at his hair.

"NOW GET YOUR HAIRY BOTTOMS ON THAT CART! IMMEDIATELY!"

Julius, Cornelius, Lucia, and Rufus all dashed to the cart, where they found Milus lounging at the back. He just tutted and shook his head at them in disbelief.

"WAIT!" cried Julius. "Where's Felix?"

From the beach came a strained cry. "JULIUS! GUYS! COME AND GIVE ME A HAND!"

"That antelope is going to get us in so much trouble," huffed Julius. "Come on, before Septimus notices."

Back on the beach, Felix was struggling with his bulging knapsack.

They all grabbed the pack and tried to lift it up, but it was impossible.

"This is ridiculous!" gasped Julius. "What have you *got* in there?"

"It's my rock collection," said Felix. "I take it everywhere I go."

"We're going to have to drag it," said Cornelius. "And be quick about it, before Septimus sees us and explodes like Mount Vesuvius."

Between them they were able to pull it over to the cart, but they still couldn't lift it onto the back.

"I'm sorry, Felix," said Julius. "But you're going to have to lose some of your rocks. You can't carry this pack around everywhere."

"NOOOO!" cried Felix. "You can't make me!" He tried again to heft his pack up, but to no avail, and he finally collapsed in a heap. A small tear trickled down his cheek.

Cornelius sat next to Felix and put his arm around him. "Come on, buddy," he said. "Maybe pick your all-time favorites and we can go from there. I bet there's some you don't really need."

Felix just sat there, looking glum. "But I love ALL my rocks."

"We can help you choose!" said Lucia. She convinced Felix to empty his knapsack and lay out all his rocks neatly on the ground. Everyone stood back and stared in awe at the strange and wonderful collection.

"To be fair," said Julius, "that *is* a pretty amazing collection!"

"We're trying to help Felix with his rock collection," said Julius. "He's having trouble deciding which ones to keep and which ones to leave behind."

Septimus grabbed a handful of the rocks, walked over to the water's edge, and hurled them into the sea.

"There," he said, brushing his hands. "Now let's MOVE IT!"

⚜CHAPTER NINE⚜
LONDINIUM CALLING

Julius gaped at the endless green fields and ancient woodlands as their cart rolled along the smooth Roman road. Occasionally, in the distance here and there, he could spot odd-looking round houses with roofs of straw and walls of mud. "Why did the Romans come to Britannia? It's just fields and trees!" said Julius. "I haven't seen one person out here yet."

"Don't worry," replied Rufus, who was keeping a watchful eye. "I'm sure we'll come across some of those gangly weirdos before you know it!"

Bored with looking at fields, Julius snuggled down among the packs and drifted off to sleep.

In his dreams he found himself being chased by a tall, scary monster.

"LEAVE ME ALONE!" cried Julius as he tried to escape through a muddy field, but the monster was fast and soon caught up with him. As Julius turned to face the monster, he noticed that it was wearing a pair of stripey pants. "HEY!" cried Julius. "Are you wearing my LEGS?"

"No!" came a familiar voice. "You're wearing *MY* LEGS!"

"Oh, BROTHER!" cried Julius. "Have you come to set me FREE?"

"DON'T LET THEM STEAL YOUR LEGS, JULIUS!" said Brutus.

"I WON'T!" cried Julius. "I WON'T LET THEM STEAL MY LEGS!"

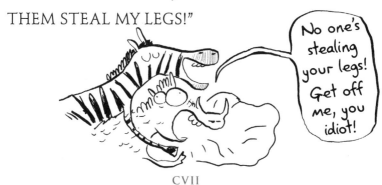

"WAKE UP, YOU LAZY BOZOS!" roared
Septimus. "WE'RE HERE!"

Through the murk of the dusk, Julius could make
out the unmistakable shapes of Roman buildings,
standing square and tall along the bank.

"Welcome to LONDINIUM!"
said Septimus.

As Julius rubbed his tired eyes, he looked out at a noisy, bustling port. His nostrils were hit by the very familiar stink of a city as the cart rumbled over a long wooden bridge that crossed a great snaking river.

"Gosh!" he said, taking in the view. "This must be where everybody was hiding. Check out all those ships!"

"Merchant ships," said Cornelius. "The Romans need their home comforts. You can bet those boats are filled with wine and olive oil and all that stinky fish sauce they pour on everything."

"It looks like they're taking lots of stuff away, too," said Julius. "Look at all those poor sheep and cows being piled onto that ship. I don't envy their ride."

"NOW you know why the Romans are here," said Cornelius. "They need to feed and clothe that growing empire of theirs."

"Keep an eye out for those vicious BRITONS, though," warned Julius, ducking down in the cart. "They're not getting MY stripey legs!"

"I think you'll find they're everywhere!" said Cornelius, smiling.

"Yeah!" said Rufus. "And you know what? They look pretty ordinary to me!"

Julius peeked out from in between the packs and stared at all the strange-looking people going about their business.

I suppose they do....

"But it's COLD!" protested Julius. "Why aren't they trying to kill us for our furs?"

"I think maybe Cornelius has been listening to too many scared Romans!" Rufus said with a laugh.

You mark my words: there's trouble to be had on this island!

"Rufus is probably right," said Julius. "We don't have a thing to worry about. This place looks as normal as anywhere! The tournament is going to be a BREEZE. Like Hadrian said, the locals will LOVE us."

After trundling through the city, the cart suddenly took a sharp left, revealing a wooden amphitheater up ahead. "OOH! I think we've found our vacation house!" squealed Julius.

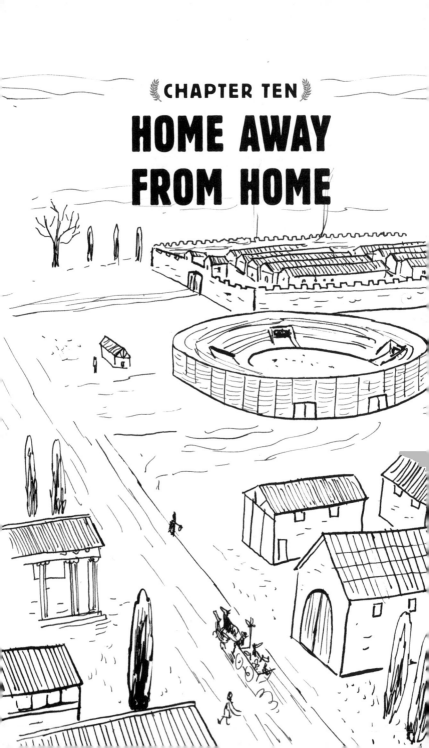

CHAPTER TEN

HOME AWAY FROM HOME

"It's a lot smaller than I expected," said Julius, looking the amphitheater up and down. "That gives me hope: their home crowd won't be anywhere near as noisy as the Colosseum's. We'll win *easily* in there!"

The small amphitheater was surrounded by fields, but just behind it sat an imposing stone fort.

"WHOA!" gasped Cornelius. "That fort must house A THOUSAND soldiers. Look at the size of it!"

Septimus laughed as he pulled the cart up next to a ramshackle old barn. "You must be JOKING if you think we're going to let a bunch of STINKING FLEABAGS LIKE YOU stay in our fort."

He grabbed their knapsacks off the cart and chucked them onto the ground.

"THIS is where YOU FOOLS are staying during your little 'vacation'!" he said with a grin.

Julius jumped off the cart, grumbling. "You can't expect us to stay in there. It's FREEZING!"

Septimus rubbed his hands together to keep warm as a biting wind blew through the city. "You'd best

cuddle up close together to keep warm tonight."
He chuckled. "I don't want any of you dying of
hypothermia—Hadrian would be VERY displeased!"

Septimus climbed back onto the cart. "Our
tournament starts in two days, so we'll have a nice
long training session tomorrow to get you warmed
up. SEE YOU AT THE CRACK OF DAWN!" With
that, he merrily trundled off toward the fort.

The sky suddenly darkened, and with a crack of
thunder, a great downpour fell on the city.

"Quick! Get inside the barn!" said Lucia.

They crashed through the rotten door to find a foul, damp hovel, strewn with moldy straw and bales of stinking hay. Rain streamed in through holes in the roof.

Great. Just great.

Milus stood up and brushed wet straw from his fur. "Well, this is just GREAT!" he growled. "When these sneaky Romans finally chuck my broken body into some cold, wet ditch somewhere, can you please make sure it says 'I TOLD YOU SO!' on my tombstone?"

Milus hurled his knapsack to the floor, and as it landed, it let out a huge squeak. Everybody turned and looked at the pack.

"I know that squeak," whispered Cornelius.

"Thanks for leaving me behind AGAIN!" he screeched. "I teach you ALL my fighting techniques, I turn you into SUPERSTARS, and what thanks do I get? NONE!" He sat down and started nibbling on a biscuit.

"Have you been in Milus's pack all this time?" said Julius.

"So what if I have?" replied Pliny, spitting crumbs everywhere. "I wasn't going to show my face and get roped into scrubbing ships' decks. Do you think I'm STUPID or something?"

"So, what's going on here, anyway?" asked Pliny. "I heard you all talking about going on vacay. Where are we? It's not warm, so it can't be Egypt."

"Britannia!" said Julius.

Pliny nearly choked on his biscuit.

"Then you've HAD it!" he cried. "This island is the LAST place you want to be!"

"But Hadrian says we're going to inspire the locals," said Julius. "He set up a tournament for us and EVERYTHING! We're the People's Champions!"

"The People's Nincompoops, more like," said Pliny. "The locals don't need entertaining; they need OVERPOWERING!"

"What do you mean?" gasped Julius.

"The Britons are on the verge of REVOLT!" said Pliny. "I heard all about it in the Colosseum. I get ALL my gossip there. The Senate is totally scared about the WHOLE situation. Hadrian is obviously using your so-called popularity as a show of his strength to shut up these whining Britons AND the senators."

"But if you guys fail to impress these barbarians and they keep on being a bunch of troublemakers, the Senate will FORCE Hadrian to start a very expensive war against Britannia."

"But we're training tomorrow," whimpered Julius. "Then our first fight is the day after. We don't have much time!"

CHAPTER ELEVEN

MUD, SWEAT, AND TEARS

The next morning, big blobs of water dripped off Julius's nose as icy rain spat down outside the wooden amphitheater. Septimus marched up and down, wrapped up warm and dry in his nice thick furs, as he inspected the line of animals.

"WHAT?" spluttered Julius. "Push-ups in this cold mud? You must be joking!"

Septimus leaned close up to Julius's face. "DO I LOOK LIKE I'M JOKING?"

"N-n-now that you mention it, no, you d-d-don't. . . ." stammered Julius.

"Good," declared Septimus. "YOU can give me a hundred!"

Julius refused to get on the ground. "This is SO unfair, Septimus. You can't make us train in this weather!"

"Yeah!" said Felix. "It's all right for *you,* wrapped up all nice and warm."

"OK," said Septimus, "then let me introduce you to an old Roman army trick for warming up." He wandered over to a patch of weeds and grabbed a big handful of nettles.

"I'm not sure I like the look of this. . . ." whispered Julius nervously.

Septimus held up the nettles. "When I was in the Tenth Legion, fighting barbarians in the FORESTS OF GERMANIA, we didn't SNIVEL about the COLD and WET!"

"What's he going to do?" whispered a perplexed Felix. "Eat them?"

"NO!" continued Septimus. "We thought on our feet. We created SOLUTIONS!" He suddenly whacked Felix's legs with the nettles.

Felix hopped around, rubbing his legs and crying in pain. "That REALLY STUNG!" he wailed.

"But aren't your legs warm now?" said Septimus.

Felix stopped leaping around and had a good look at his red, throbbing legs.

"We're warm! We're warm!" shrieked Cornelius as they all sprinted off across the field.

"Well," said Septimus, "seeing as you're all running already, I want you to jog around the fort, up to the river, then back here again."

"EXACTLY!" barked Septimus. "CHOP, CHOP! Get moving, you lazy donkey!"

The animals ran off toward the fort behind the amphitheater, huffing and puffing as they went.

"I hate running!" spluttered Felix. "I've got flat hooves."

"I'm still exhausted after our training with Pliny last night. I can barely feel my claws!" moaned Lucia.

Julius suddenly sprinted past them all.

Everyone ran up to the strange hut with its pointy straw roof and tiny door.

"Do you think there's anyone inside?" asked Julius.

"I saw smoke coming out of the top of the roof, so there must be," said Lucia.

"But what if it's those scary warriors from the woods?" asked Felix.

"They were going in the complete opposite direction," said Rufus.

"Oh, yeah," replied Felix, and he nudged the door open.

Felix poked his head in, and let out an ENORMOUS SCREAM, causing everyone else to scream, too. They all ran away from the hut as fast as their legs could carry them.

"COME BACK!" yelled Julius to Felix. "WHY ARE WE RUNNING AWAY?"

"I SAW SOMETHING MOVE!" Felix screeched.

Suddenly, he smacked right into a big wet lump standing in the middle of the field.

"SEPTIMUS!"

"Quite correct, imbecile!" growled Septimus, rain dripping down his angry red face. "And you're going to regret EVER running away!"

❧CHAPTER TWELVE❧
BRITONS GOT TALENT

The next morning, the animals got up at sunrise and dashed to the wooden arena, where Septimus was waiting for them.

"EVERYBODY ON THE FLOOR AND GIVE ME ONE HUNDRED PUSH-UPS!"

As they sprang into action, Septimus marched up and down sternly.

"Now you listen to me, you DEADBEATS!"

Everyone looked up, but no one dared to stop their exercises.

"Today is the first day of our glorious TOURNAMENT! Hadrian has chosen you idiots, FOOLISHLY, to my mind, to REPRESENT ROME against the BRITONS!"

Lucia put up her claw. Septimus spun around and glared at the crocodile. "This had better be GOOD!" he said through his gritted teeth.

Septimus's eyes nearly popped out with rage. He thrust his stick in her belly. "You. Give me one hundred jumping jacks! NOW!"

Septimus continued with his speech. "You'll be up against Britannia's GREATEST animal gladiators, and I'm expecting YOU to prove Rome's MIGHT and send them packing, thus soothing the BRITONS' angry little brains and eradicating any thoughts they might have about rising up against their wonderful Roman benefactors. UNDERSTAND?"

Benefactors?
Don't you mean
"evil conquerors"?

Septimus picked Felix up by the scruff of his neck. "You do realize that GERMANIA is a lot farther from here than it is from Rome? I'm going to have to kick your backside EVEN HARDER to get you there if you don't shut up WITH YOUR BABBLING!"

"So sorry, Septimus," whimpered Felix. "Would you like me to give you another hundred push-ups?"

Septimus dropped Felix back on the ground. "That would be very kind of you, thank you."

"Now, this tournament begins in TWO HOURS," roared Septimus, "so I want you dressed and ready for combat in ONE! Do NOT be late!" And he stalked off to the Roman fort.

The animals flopped to the floor, exhausted. But before they had a chance to catch their breath, Pliny the mouse scuttled into view.

"Oh, look out!" said Julius.

"YES, 'LOOK OUT,' INDEED!" snapped the tiny mouse.

"What was THAT for?" shouted Julius.

"'WHAT WAS THAT FOR?' You abandoned me in Rome, then you abandon me in this crazy place. What's *wrong* with me? Do I smell of *cheese* or something?"

"A little," said Julius, rubbing his shin.

Cornelius kicked Julius on his other leg. "Shush!"

"We don't know what we're up against here," squeaked Pliny, "so let's make sure we're ready for ANYTHING!"

CHAPTER THIRTEEN

PIGS MIGHT FLY

With the tournament minutes away from starting, the arena was already packed with a mix of Roman dignitaries and rowdy Britons.

Julius and Cornelius peeked through the gateway to check out the audience.

Cornelius looked toward the north entrance of the arena, where their opponents would appear from. "I wonder who we're up against. I gotta say, I really don't like my chances against a bear."

See any half-naked savages?

Not yet...

A big hand slapped onto Cornelius's shoulder.

"FEAR NOT, WARTHOG!" barked Septimus. "We have a special adversary for you, Piggy!"

The *cornicines* suddenly blared their horns to declare that the games had begun.

"Good luck, Cornelius!" said Julius. "Show those Brits who's boss!"

"Yeah! Kick some Briton BUTT!" yelled Pliny.

The *summa rudis* marched into the center of the arena and raised his arms to silence the crowd.

"CITIZENS OF THE ROMAN EMPIRE!" he

cried. A wave of angry BOOs rippled around the arena. The *summa rudis* let out a nervous cough. "Welcome to BRITONS GOT TALENT, where we pit ROMAN versus BRITON, as we bring you CHAMPIONS from the city of Rome itself!"

"In our first fight today," continued the *summa rudis,* "we will witness PIG VERSUS PIG!"

"WHAT?" cried Cornelius. "I . . . I don't understand. . . ."

A bloodthirsty cheer erupted around the tiny stadium.

"What sort of pigs do they have out here, then?" asked Julius.

"Uh, THAT sort!" said Felix, pointing to the other end of the arena.

"FLIPPIN' HECK! He's like a shaved version of Cornelius!" said Rufus.

"From Britannia," continued the *summa rudis,* "we have PERICLES THE PIG!" A great roar went up, shaking the wooden structure of the stadium. "And from Rome, CORNELIUS THE WARTHOG!"

Cornelius stumbled out to the center of the arena to a mix of cheers and boos.

Pericles the pig looked unimpressed. "Not *him*!" he growled. "I want the zebra!"

The *summa rudis* tried to placate him. "I'm afraid you don't understand, Pericles. There isn't a *choice* of opponent. You have to fight the warthog."

"No, Roman, YOU don't understand!"

The crowd rose to their feet as Pericles confronted poor Cornelius. "And that means YOU, TOO, ROMAN HOG!"

The enraged Pericles stood bellowing and snorting at the Roman arena gate. "THE ZEBRA!" he roared. "BRING ME THE ZEBRA! I WILL BRING YOU ROMANS DOWN!"

"Well, that's a good start," said Julius with a gulp.

The agitated crowd started booing and chanting, "ROMANS OUT! ROMANS OUT!"

Septimus signaled to two watching soldiers to drag Pericles away.

"No, Donkey, it is NOT a good start," growled Septimus.

"Maybe I should go on next, to calm the crowd," said Julius. "Who's the next opponent?"

"Douglas the sheep," replied Septimus.

"A SHEEP?" Felix laughed. "Sheep are stupid, bumbling creatures!"

SKIP!

Leave this to ME!

"WAIT!" cried Septimus. "THIS IS NO ORDINARY SHEEP. . . . " But it was too late. Felix skipped into the arena, greeted by boos and laughter.

The blast of the *cornicines'* horns and the roar of the crowd signaled the entrance of Felix's opponent.

"AAIIEE! YOU'RE NOT A *SHEEP*!" screamed
Felix. "YOU'RE A *MONSTER*!"

"ARE YE THE ZEBRA?" growled Douglas,
thumping his shield against his horns like a drum.

"Um . . . no," whimpered Felix. "I'm the antelope."

"Then YER GOIN' DOWN, ROMAN!"

The crowd roared their approval.

Back at the gate, Julius put his head in his hooves.

"This really isn't going to end well."

The *cornicines* signaled the start of the fight, and the
grizzled sheep didn't waste any time in battering his
sword against Felix's shield.

Much to everyone's surprise, the plucky antelope held his ground against the relentless blows.

But suddenly the sheep jogged away to the far side of the arena. Julius turned to Pliny and the others and shrugged. "Where's he going?"

"Maybe these Britons aren't as tough as we thought," Pliny said with a laugh. "Felix has got him on the run!"

"I wouldn't bet on it," warned Milus.

Douglas the sheep bent forward, pointing his unwieldy horns in Felix's direction, and bellowed, "YE ROMANS CAN'T PUSH US AROUND ANYMORE! YE ARE GOING DOWN!"

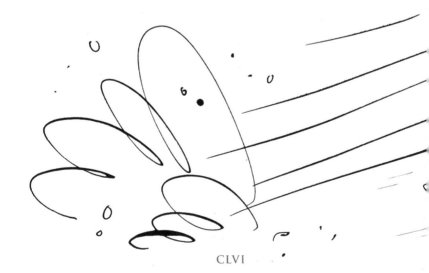

The crowd stood up and cheered their approval.

A furious and desperate Septimus turned to Julius.
"GET OUT THERE, DONKEY!" he screamed.
"Fight for the pride of Rome! And if you DON'T win,
YOU AND YOUR PATHETIC FRIENDS WILL
NEVER SEE FREEDOM AGAIN!"

CHAPTER FOURTEEN

HOO NOO, BROON COO!

Septimus shoved Julius out into the arena. "NOW, MAKE YOUR EMPEROR PROUD!" he bellowed.

A great roar erupted from the crowd as Julius strutted to the center of the arena.

In Rome only a few weeks ago, Julius had entered the Colosseum the people's hero, but out here it was a different story entirely; out here the audience saw Julius as the enemy and hated him and all his fellow Roman gladiators.

He'd already seen Cornelius and Felix soundly thrashed by the ferocious Britons. He was going to have to draw on all his training and experience to get him through the next few minutes.

Go on, Julius!

Knock some sense into these barbarians!

Back at the gate, Lucia, Rufus, Milus, and Pliny looked on anxiously.

"This crowd REALLY hates us," said Rufus.

"Actually, they hate the Romans, and that includes US!" replied Lucia, biting her claws.

"I'm not sure I like being called a Roman," whispered Rufus, trying not to let Septimus hear him.

"Me neither," said Lucia.

"We'll let Julius fight this next gladiator, then we'll make a run for it," whispered Rufus.

"Good idea," said Lucia. "I'll start thinking of an escape plan. You in, Milus?"

The familiar PARP of the *cornicines'* horns finally heralded the entrance of Julius's opponent.

"ALL THE WAY FROM THE HIGHLANDS OF CALEDONIA," cried the *summa rudis,* "BERTA THE COW!"

From the opposite gate stomped in the biggest, hairiest cow Julius or any of the others had ever seen.

"GEEZ!" cried Pliny. "Look at the horns on HER!"

As the *summa rudis* drew the two adversaries together, Julius gasped at the size of his opponent.

"Are YE supposed to be THE MIGHTY ZEEBRA?" rasped Berta, poking Julius in the stomach. "Ye dunna look so mighty from where AH'M standin'!"

The trumpets signaled the start of the fight, and Julius immediately shoved the huge cow with his shield, forcing her to stumble backward. The audience let out a gasp.

The embarrassed Berta held up her massive two-handed sword above her head and rushed at Julius with a great ROAR, then brought the blade down onto Julius's shield with a KLANG, sending thundering shockwaves through his body.

KLANG!

"Yikes! I felt THAT!" shuddered Pliny.

"I think the whole amphitheater did," said Lucia, peeking through her claws.

Berta unleashed a volley of blows against the valiant but ultimately overpowered zebra, pinning him to the floor.

"Haven't yez got it into yer head yet, Zeebra?" spat Berta. "We DUNNA WANT yez Romans here!"

"I don't want to be here, EITHER!" cried Julius.

The crowd was going wild. Some of them even started ripping up the wooden stadium seats and chucking the broken slats into the arena.

Septimus had seen enough.

Gathering all his strength, Julius let out a great yell.
He charged at the enormous cow with his shield and
flew into an attack with his sword, but Berta easily
parried him away, sending Julius crashing to the
ground.

Julius leaped up, but with a swipe of the handle of her sword, Berta sent him flying, knocking his helmet right off his head.

The cow raised her massive sword for one final blow.

The dazed Julius braced himself behind his shield, his energy and resolve finally spent.

"JULIUS! NOOOOO!" cried a desperate Lucia.

The whole arena exploded with a deep roar from the crowd. The empire's so-called great zebra champion and ALL the Roman gladiators were BEATEN!

Some of the audience began climbing over the arena wall and chanting abuse at the Roman dignitaries. Big chunks of wooden seating rained down, sending the Romans running for their lives.

The unruly crowd then turned on the handful of cowering Roman soldiers who were struggling to keep the situation under control.

"GET THAT STRIPEY IDIOT BACK HERE AT ONCE!" Septimus screamed.

Rufus and Lucia sprinted to their stricken friend, who lay semiconscious on the arena floor, the rampaging crowd threatening to trample him underfoot.

Let's get him out of here quickly!

Septimus shepherded them all out the back gate and straight into the Roman fort next door as the amphitheater erupted into chaos.

After the giant gates of the fort slammed shut behind them, Septimus exploded into a frenzy.

"HADRIAN WILL BE HEARING ABOUT THIS OUTRAGE!" he yelled. "IN FACT, I'VE GOT A GOOD MIND TO SEND YOU ALL PACKING BACK TO ROME!"

He grabbed Julius and pulled him right up to his face.

"You have another fight in two days, Donkey. Prepare to be trained to within an inch of YOUR MISERABLE, FURRY LIFE!"

CHAPTER FIFTEEN

HOLE LOT OF TROUBLE

The next morning, Septimus put Julius and his friends through their most punishing training regime EVER.

Felix was really starting to struggle. "THESE PUSH-UPS ARE KILLING ME!" he cried. "I CAN'T FEEL MY ARMS!"

Septimus stormed over. "What's that, Goat? You can't feel your arms, you say?"

"No . . ." whimpered the floundering antelope.

"Then let's work on those RIDICULOUS SPINDLY LEGS OF YOURS!"

Soon they all collapsed from exhaustion, dizziness, and discombobulation.

"GOOD WORK!" barked Septimus. "Have a little rest, because we're off for a twenty-mile cross-country run in five minutes."

"We don't stand a chance against those Briton beasts no matter HOW much we train!" whimpered Felix. "I don't know what they eat out here, but they're MONSTERS!"

Lucia sidled up to Julius. "Fear not," she whispered. "I have formulated an escape plan!" And she tapped the side of her nose.

"But how?" said Julius. "Septimus will be watching us like a hawk after last time."

"Don't worry," she said, tapping her nose again. "Just watch me."

"No dressing up?"

"No dressing up!" the crocodile promised.

Septimus looked at Lucia suspiciously. "WAIT A MINUTE!" he said. "You must think I'm STUPID!"

"Whatever do you mean?" replied Lucia innocently.

"If you think I'm going to let you go running on your own after LAST TIME, you've got another thing coming. I'm going with you!"

"Of course!" said Lucia, and they all ran off toward the fort.

As they reached the fort, Lucia jogged up next to Septimus.

"So, have you had much of a chance to look around Britannia since we arrived, Septimus?" she asked politely.

"WHAT?" replied Septimus gruffly. "No, I haven't, not while I've had to keep an eye on YOU ODDBALLS!"

"Oh, it really *is* a lovely place," she said. "Rolling hills and beautiful meadows to rival even Rome itself."

"In fact, the wet seasons here create a *gorgeous* lush green landscape."

"SHOW ME these meadows, Crocodile," said Septimus. "I do like collecting wildflowers. They can often be useful ingredients for the infusion of balms and oils."

Lucia winked at the others.

"He does like his bathing oils, old Septimus," whispered Julius.

As they trotted across the fields and around marshlands, Lucia dutifully pointed out interesting plants and natural wonders.

They skirted around the edge of the ancient woodlands, keeping a beady eye out for any shifty-looking warriors who might jump out with their bows and arrows.

Finally, they reached the boggy puddles that Rufus had cleverly steered the gang through while escaping the local barbarians.

"Yes, good plan!" agreed Septimus, admiring the view. "And when we get back, we can finish off with FIFTY JUMPING JACKS!"

"But Septimus, we can jump *here*!" cried Lucia.

"Yes, that looks like oodles of fun!" said Felix, and he and Rufus both joined in, leaping from puddle to puddle.

"Come on, Julius and Cornelius!" called out Lucia with a cheeky wink. "And you, Milus. You could definitely do with some cheering up!"

"YOUR TURN!" shouted Lucia to Septimus.

Septimus huffed with indignation. "You are, of course, joking."

"Oh, come on, Septimus!" cried Felix. "Jump away all that tension! No one's looking!"

Septimus grimaced, his eyes swiveling from one side to the other, to see if anyone might actually be watching. He took a deep breath and snorted through his big hairy nostrils.

"Oh, all right," he muttered.

"SEE?" shouted Lucia. "I told you!"

As Septimus gleefully hopped from one big puddle to the next, Lucia suddenly pointed to a MASSIVE puddle just up ahead. "Check out the size of THAT one!" she squealed. "YOU have it, Septimus."

"OF *COURSE* I SHOULD HAVE IT!" he bellowed. And he took an enormous run before leaping into the air like a gazelle.

"I KNOW!" cried Lucia. "That's the puddle Rufus fell into up to his neck! I saved it especially for Septimus!"

"QUICKLY!" shouted Julius. "Let's move it before he surfaces!" And they ran away as fast as they could.

As they leaped over hedges and across fields, Cornelius suddenly slapped his face.

"PLINY!" he cried. "We forgot PLINY again!"

"No, we didn't," said Milus, and he opened a pouch attached to his belt.

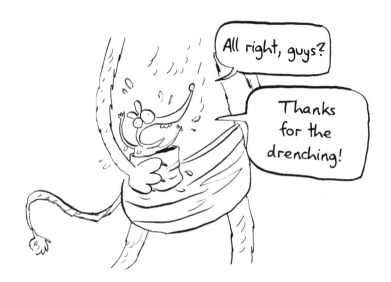

"Lucia warned me about her plan, and I thought we should probably bring the little rodent along for the ride," said Milus.

"What?" said Julius, confused. "You *knew* about the puddle plan beforehand?"

"You think I'd be happily jumping in puddles otherwise?" Milus snarled.

"Hmm . . . I *did* wonder!" said Felix.

"And do you have a plan as to what we do NOW, Lucia?" squeaked Cornelius. "We're in the middle of nowhere!"

"Follow me!" she said before jogging off.

As they followed her over a hill, Lucia pointed to a familiar-looking round hut with smoke drifting out of its tall, pointed roof.

"We're staying here tonight!" said the crocodile. "They'll never think of looking for us here." Lucia ran up to the small door and gave it a gentle knock.

"But there's a GHOST living in there!" screamed Felix, backing away slowly. "I saw it with my own eyeballs!"

"You saw no such thing," said Milus.

"But what if it's the home of ANGRY BARBARIAN WARRIORS?" asked a worried Julius.

"Then we just look for somewhere else to stay," replied Lucia, shrugging. "Simple!"

Suddenly, the little wooden door creaked open, and a strange, pungent smell wafted out of the hut.

A hooded old lady shuffled into the doorway. "Do come in," she said with a smile. "I've just been cooking a broth. . . ."

CHAPTER SIXTEEN
BOIL AND BUBBLE

"Why are we here?" whispered Julius, looking around the eerie hovel. "This place gives me the CREEPS!"

"You are free to leave," croaked the old lady. "Do you think me glad to have the likes of a lion and a crocodile prowling about my house?"

"Y-yeah, she's right." Felix gulped. "We should go and find somewhere else to sleep. I'll see you guys later. . . ."

"You're going nowhere," said Rufus, pulling Felix back by the horns.

"Please excuse my friends," apologized Lucia. "We're just looking for somewhere to spend the night."

"I *know* who you are!" said the old crone, turning toward the warthog and staring deep into his eyes. "You are *Romans,* but I believe there is more to you than meets the eye."

She shuffled to the middle of the room, where a large iron cauldron bubbled away, the source of the overpowering stench. "I have been making a broth. You are most welcome to partake with me."

She immediately coughed and retched, spitting the broth back into the cauldron. "Needs more salt," she said, and shuffled to one of her shelves to pick up a small bowl of salt crystals.

Felix made a face of disgust at Julius, sticking out his tongue. "I ain't eating it," he whispered. "You can't *make* me!"

Lucia gave the antelope a swift kick in the shin to shut him up.

"I heard word of your contest yesterday. There is much trouble in the air," croaked the old lady as she handed out bowls of broth.

The Romans are weak ... and the people can tell.

"We were brought over here to demonstrate how strong Rome is," said Julius helpfully.

"A last throw of the dice from a weak emperor!" rasped the old lady. "War is coming and he knows it. We all know it. And there's nothing Hadrian can do to stop it."

"That's what I'VE been trying to tell 'em!" piped up Pliny, poking his head out of Milus's pouch. "These Romans are SCOUNDRELS. I wouldn't trust them as far as I could THROW them!"

The old lady laughed at the feisty mouse.

"Would you like some broth, too, little warrior? I have plenty to go around."

"Will you, now?" growled Milus.

"Excuse me, but if the Romans are so weak," said Julius as he sipped his broth, "then what do any of you have to fear?"

The old crone stared into the hearth. "Our own leaders are weak, too! We have plenty of fighting men, but they are a rabble without leadership."

What we need is a chieftain.

Someone like Boudicca!

"Boudicca?" said Julius. "Who's Boudicca?"

Ahem!
Boudicca is the warrior queen who nearly defeated the Romans sixty years ago!

"Your hairy friend knows his history well!" the old lady said appreciatively. "I was at the warrior queen's side when we nearly drove these Roman cockroaches away all those years ago."

"WOW! How exciting!" exclaimed Lucia.

The crone continued. "So *fearsome* was our queen that she almost rid every nook and cranny of our land of these vermin. The mad Emperor Nero himself was ready to order his army's retreat and leave us as they had found us." She let out a deep sigh and shook her head. "But 'twas not to be. . . ."

The crone stood up to collect the empty bowls. "If Boudicca could see how our chieftains crawl and bow to the Roman invaders today," she rasped, "she would *rip out her own heart*!"

"Seems a bit drastic," whispered Felix to Julius.

"Please, tell us more about Boudicca," urged Lucia. "She sounds FIERCE!"

"Oh, my dear, Boudicca was a warrior so brave and ingenious, why, when she flew into battle on her chariot—"

"SHE RODE A CHARIOT?"

gasped Lucia. "By the gods, I love her ALREADY!"

Lucia nearly fainted. "Oh, but I couldn't, it's too precious."

The old crone shuffled over to the cloak and unhooked it. "Put it on, child. Our queen would share her mantle with one so courageous."

Lucia held the soft woolen cloak out in front of her. The orange and red checks looked as fresh as they must have on the day it was made. She swept it behind her and tied two corners around her neck.

Wow! It's so beautiful!

She started skipping around the room. "I want to be a queen riding into battle on my chariot!"

The old lady chuckled. "Oh, *how* we Britons need another Boudicca today!"

"HEY! I want to dress up, too!" said Julius. "But I want some of those blue paintings on my skin like our opponents!"

The old lady tottered to one of her shelves. "Then I have just the thing for you!"

She showed Julius a pot of blue paste. "This is *woad*. It is what our warriors use to paint patterns onto their bodies. Would you like to try some?"

"You must choose an animal whose image would provoke FEAR in your enemies!" said the old lady.

Felix piped up. "Make it a SPIDER, Julius. I hate spiders!"

"Good answer. A spider it is, then!" said Julius.

The crone cackled, then dipped her finger in the paste and started drawing on Julius's chest.

After ten minutes, she sat back and admired her handiwork. "Well, what do you think?"

"Then why *don't* you?" said the old lady.

"What do you mean?" said Julius.

"TAKE ON THE WORLD!" She clapped. "Bearing the drawings of these creatures gives you their POWER! You can be UNBEATABLE!"

She gathered the animals around her and whispered to them. "You'll find that Pericles, Douglas, and Berta are really no different from you; they're slaves just as much as you are. Go back and show Londinium who you REALLY are."

"You might find that you'll make more friends than enemies AND rid us of the Roman scourge once and for all!"

CHAPTER SEVENTEEN

WHEN IN LONDINIUM

The next day, with the words of the old lady ringing in their ears, Julius and his friends headed back to Londinium and the eager crowds of the amphitheater. This time they were determined to carry out what Hadrian and Septimus had demanded of them—to win over the Briton crowd. But this time it would be on their OWN terms.

"I ought to have you ARRESTED for leaving me in that big puddle yesterday," growled Septimus.

"MOVE IT," said Julius as he pushed past the *lanista*. "We're here to do our job!"

The animals strode to the arena, and Septimus did a double take at their tattoo-covered bodies.

Hey!

What's the meaning of this NONSENSE?

The *cornicines'* horns blared triumphantly, heralding the arrival of the Roman champions.

Julius and his tattooed friends burst defiantly out into the arena to a great ROAR of approval from the crowd.

Pericles, Douglas, and Berta looked on, astonished.

In the center of the arena, the *summa rudis* gathered
all the gladiators.

"WHO IS TO FIGHT FIRST?"

"I'll go first," growled Milus.

"Then so shall I," rasped Douglas the sheep.

The other gladiators dispersed to their gates,
and the two animals sized each other up. Douglas

prodded the drawing on Milus's chest with his sword. "And what's that WEE BEASTIE meant to be, then?"

The *cornicines* blared and the crowd cheered as the fight began.

The brutish sheep wasted no time in thrusting his sword toward Milus, but the nimble lion easily dodged out of the way of the deadly blade.

"Ye know, Romans wearing woad tattoos is a GREAT INSULT to my people!" spat Douglas.

"We're no different from you!" roared Milus. "We're SLAVES of the Roman Empire, too!"

"'No different'?" Douglas laughed as he lunged with his sword. "What are ye even TALKING about?"

Milus pole-vaulted on his trident and kicked the confused sheep's shield out of his hoof.

"We want to HELP you!" said Milus. He thrust his trident at Douglas's sword and wrenched it away from the sheep.

"Ye've got a funny way of showing it!" wheezed Douglas as Milus stood on him, triumphant.

The crowd leaped to their feet. Their own champion might have been beaten, but he'd been beaten by another renegade of the empire!

Pericles the pig flew into a rage. "I'M NOT PUTTING UP WITH THIS NONSENSE!" he cried, and raced to the center of the arena.

"I'd better go out there and face him," said Julius, marching out to great cheers and whistles from the crowd.

In the wings, Septimus was FURIOUS.
"WHAT ARE YOU IMBECILES UP TO? YOU'RE
SUPPOSED TO SHUT THE CROWD UP, NOT
MAKE THEM *WORSE*!"

The *summa rudis* signaled for the fight to begin,
and Pericles hammered down ax blows onto Julius's
shield. "We're not falling for your TRICKERY,
Zebra!" he cried out. "We are NOT to be fooled in
Britannia. We know you Romans too well!"

"LIES!" cried the pig.

Julius leaped into the air like the spider tattooed on his chest and clonked Pericles on the back of his head.

"JOIN US!" he said to Pericles. "We can take down the Roman Army TOGETHER!"

"Why should we join up with WEAKLINGS? We can take on the Roman Army without you!"

Pericles didn't have an answer. Julius saw that the pig was momentarily troubled by his taunt and attacked him while he was distracted.

"You knew who I was before I even came here!" cried Julius as he bashed against the pig's axes. "You know what I'm capable of. If I can beat the best in Rome, together WE can be rid of the Roman curse from Britannia!"

Julius stood, triumphant, and raised his sword into the air.

He turned to the red-faced Septimus and gestured to the chanting crowd. "Consider your Britons WON OVER!" he cried.

Suddenly, out of the blue, a barrage of trumpets sounded, and a legion of soldiers poured into the arena. A standard-bearer followed, leading a golden chariot pulled by two magnificent white horses. Standing triumphantly on the chariot was Emperor Hadrian himself!

"HADRIAN? HERE?" Julius cried. "I don't understand!"

"You disappoint me!" said Hadrian. "My own champion A TRAITOR!"

CHAPTER EIGHTEEN

HE CAME, HE SAW, HE LOCKED HIM UP

"Take him and his friends and throw them into the dungeon!" commanded Hadrian.

"You're not the emperor here, Hadrian!" said Julius defiantly as he was dragged away. "These woad-wearing warriors will rise up and defeat you!"

"SILENCE!" snapped Hadrian. "As a SLAVE of Rome, your words are meaningless."

"While you were out here, plotting with your traitorous friends, our new People's Champion has received special intense training from Victorius himself!"

Hadrian laughed at Julius's confused face. "He's far more loyal to the empire than you'll ever be, Zebra. He doesn't bleat ON and ON demanding his freedom; he WANTS to fight for Rome!"

He leaned in close to Julius's face. "You shall meet him when you battle him TO THE DEATH at my GRAND NEW PROJECT!"

"New project? Have you built yourself another golden toilet?" scoffed Julius.

"ALL WILL QUAKE WHEN THEY BEAR WITNESS TO ROME'S GREATEST CONSTRUCTION YET," declared Hadrian.

"Wait, did Hadrian *really* just get excited about a wall?" whispered Felix.

"These Romans are a funny lot," said Cornelius.

The animals were taken down into the dungeons of the Roman fort. As the big metal door clanged shut, Julius let out a deep sigh.

Well, THAT didn't quite work out how I expected.

"I think Hadrian turning up surprised everyone, even Septimus," said Cornelius.

Suddenly there came a scurrying noise under the door. A little head popped out through the gap.

"Have you come to rescue us?" asked Felix excitedly.

"Er, nope," said Pliny as he squished his whole body under the door. "But I *have* come bearing good news!

"I was having a chat with those weird Briton gladiators, and it seems you and Milus have successfully sown the seeds of rebellion in their minds.

"Turns out that old lady was right! Their representatives are either useless or in the pockets of the Romans, so you're *exactly* the sort of hero they can get behind!"

"You know, I've always said there was something special about you, Julius. You're going to have to be the one who takes the bull by the horns yet again!"

"HEY! I'm not fighting that big cow again, am I?" said Julius.

"No, Berta is right behind you!" replied Pliny.

"So who IS this new champion?" asked Cornelius.

"No idea!" said Pliny. "Hadrian is keeping his new pet completely under wraps. Which means we have to make sure Julius is in the best shape EVER to thrash this mystery champion, so we can show the Romans WHO'S BOSS!"

CHAPTER NINETEEN

FINAL FRONTIER

The next morning, Julius and the rest of the gladiators were shoved into wooden carts and carried off to the wilds of the northern frontier.

For three long days, they endured being cramped up in their boxes. The farther north they traveled, the colder it got and the wetter it got.

On the third day, Lucia suddenly cried out in excitement. "Look!" she shouted. "THE WALL! I can see the wall!"

Everyone craned their necks out of their cages to try to catch a glimpse of Hadrian's latest project.

"Well, that IS a big old wall," said Julius.

"So many ROCKS!" yelled Felix.

Their carts trundled over a bridge and headed toward a great fort that sat at the foot of the wall.

They passed through a huge stone gatehouse and into a busy courtyard teeming with soldiers.

"Well, did you see it?" said Hadrian. "What did you think? Isn't my wall MAGNIFICENT?"

"All I care about is finding out who this gladiator I'm up against is!" said Julius.

"All in good time, Zebra!" replied Hadrian. "One thing you can be sure about is that he is a *fearsome warrior* and your death tomorrow will be swift!"

As Julius and the others were thrown into another dungeon, Pliny sneaked in carrying a pot of blue paint. "OK, we need to get this People's Champion ready for battle!" he squeaked. Pliny dipped his paw into the paste. "What animal do you want?"

How about a warrior mouse this time? Seems appropriate!

GOOD choice!

CHAPTER TWENTY

HADRIAN'S BRAWL

Julius and the others were taken from their dungeon to the wooden amphitheater outside the wall. Inside, the thousand seats had been easily filled with the Roman soldiers who served the fort.

Hadrian took his seat alongside Septimus in the royal box. Once settled, he signaled to the *summa rudis* to let the game begin.

"Good luck, Julius!" said Cornelius, giving him a big hug. "The gods are watching over you!"

"Yeah! Good luck, Julius!" called out Pliny. "Go kick some—" Suddenly he choked on his words as he saw exactly who it was that Julius was up against. "ZEBRA BUTT?"

Julius could barely believe his eyes. "But HOW?"

Brutus skipped around, flicking his sword in the air. "Word got to me about your star status in Rome, so I thought I'd come and get a taste of the action myself!"

He sauntered up to Julius and poked his sword into his brother's chin.

"Turns out I'm a better fighter than you!"

"I find that VERY hard to believe!" cried Julius, swatting Brutus's sword away.

"Victorius HIMSELF told me, and HE should know. He's fought LOTS of gladiators. Nice work beating Victorius, by the way — that *is* quite an achievement." Brutus flicked his sword again, millimeters away from Julius's face. "But the difference between me and you is that I'M not a GREAT BIG CRYBABY!"

Brutus let out a great big laugh. "I always KNEW you were a huge loser!"

In the wings, Julius's friends were in total shock. They'd heard that his brother Brutus was a bit of a rascal, but they'd never realized he was quite so mean!

"It must be the Romans talking," said Cornelius. "If he's been hanging around with Victorius, no wonder he's gone nuts!"

In the arena, the *summa rudis* separated the two zebras. "Calm down, you two. We haven't even started yet! Wait for my signal."

He held up his stick, waited a few seconds, then brought it down: the fight had officially begun.

Julius immediately took up a defensive position. His brother's swagger told him that Brutus would be overconfident and try for an early win.

Brutus predictably went for the kill, slashing and bashing away at Julius's shield, but Julius held his ground.

From behind his shield, as powerful blows rained down on him, Julius tried to reason with his errant brother.

"I'm not YOU, Brother!" cried Brutus as he twirled in the air, showing off his new sword skills. "I'VE been promised a huge villa in the hills of Rome when I thrash you!"

Julius pushed out with his shield, causing Brutus to stumble.

"They promised me MY FREEDOM!" he cried. "And look where that got me!"

Brutus paused for a second, taking in what his brother had just said, but he immediately put it out of his mind.

"No, Brutus! They will chew you up and spit you out! Come with us. Help win our freedom and the freedom of ALL these barbarian Britons! You know I'm right!"

Julius let out a big sigh. "Well, I tried my best," he said.

Brutus hung back, confused. "What do you mean, you tried your best?"

Julius didn't give him time to think. He leaped into a somersault, landed behind his bewildered brother, and smacked him across the back of the head, knocking him out cold.

In the royal box, Hadrian was livid with fury. This was NOT the outcome he'd been promised!

Hadrian's guards grabbed Julius as the emperor raged in his box. "SEIZE THE OTHER BEASTS, TOO! DON'T LET ANY OF THEM ESCAPE!"

As Julius was being dragged away, one of Hadrian's soldiers approached the royal box. "Caesar, the other animals are nowhere to be seen!"

"NOWHERE?" cried Hadrian. "That's ridiculous. Where were all my guards?"

"Er . . ." The soldier coughed nervously. "Watching your gladiators, sir."

"WAIT! SOLDIER!" cried the emperor. "BRING ME MY SNAKES AND A WINE SACK! I will show these BEASTS that I will NOT BE TRIFLED WITH! Bring the zebra with you!"

At the bottom of the fort was a wide, fast-running, twisting river. "You are trouble, Zebra," muttered Hadrian, "and there's only one way we Romans deal with troublemakers."

Two soldiers ran up to the emperor and presented him with a large sack, a wooden box, and a pair of big leather gloves.

Hadrian put on the gloves and opened the box.

There you are, my pretties!

He carefully picked up one of the snakes by the back of its neck, then gestured to one of the soldiers. "Open the bag and make the zebra stand in it!"

"HEY! What are you up to, YOU WEIRDO?" cried Julius.

The two legionnaires wrestled poor Julius, his arms still tied behind his back, into the sack. Hadrian smiled as he dropped a squirming snake into the sack.

The second snake was a little harder to get hold of, but Hadrian deftly grabbed it and released it into the sack.

Julius tried to stay calm as the snakes wriggled around his hooves. "The people of Rome WON'T be happy when they discover what you've done with me!" he bluffed. "You have a fight on your hands here, and you'll have one at home, too!"

"Oh, get over yourself!" snapped Hadrian. "You're not that important. Champion gladiators come and go like the wind." He gestured to the soldiers. "Sew this windbag up!"

The soldiers pulled the sack over Julius's head and quickly stitched it up.

"NOW THROW HIM IN THE RIVER, AND LET'S GET OUT OF HERE."

CHAPTER TWENTY-ONE

HE AIN'T HEAVY . . .

Julius tried not to panic. Although, to be fair, there was plenty to panic about. He was stuck in a sack with two venomous snakes, and they'd just been thrown into the river. He'd been in scrapes before, but this one was . . . well, scrapier.

Julius decided that he would try to reason with the snakes. "Now, listen, guys, we're in a bit of a tight situation here, so let's try to not get too bitey, OK?"

"Er, excuse me," said the other snake. "Are you by any chance JULIUS Zebra?"

"Um . . . why, yes, I am, actually," replied Julius.

Omigosh! I am SUCH a big fan!

"R-really . . . ?" stammered Julius.

"Tell him, Annie. Tell him I'm a big fan!"

"He's a big fan! In fact, we're BOTH big fans! Although Tybalt here has seen more of your fights in Rome than I have."

"It's AMAZING to see you so close up!" gushed Tybalt. "You're normally so tiny and far away!"

"Oh, well," said Julius, getting all bashful, "I do hope I'm not a disappointment." He brushed his mane with his hoof.

"Sorry to be embarrassing," said Annie, "but can we have your hoofprint?"

Before Julius could answer, their sack suddenly jolted hard, and Julius and the snakes were thrown from one end to the other.

And with a great thud, they landed on very hard ground.

Outside the bag, Julius could hear a frantic voice.

"PLEASE BE ALIVE! PLEASE BE ALIVE! I'VE BEEN SUCH AN IDIOT!"

With a great *rrrip,* the top of the sack was pulled open, and Julius and the two snakes flopped onto the grass.

Julius looked up to see his brother, Brutus. "Yes, you HAVE been an idiot," he said.

"YOU'RE ALIVE!" screamed Brutus. "The snakes didn't kill you!"

"Big fans of mine, apparently!" said Julius.

Gasp!

I still can't believe I shared a sack with JULIUS ZEBRA!

The greatest day of my life!

Brutus gave Julius a big hug. "I'm so sorry, Julius. Once I saw what they were going to do to you, I knew those Romans were RASCALS, just like you said!"

Julius let out a great big sigh. "So you didn't figure that out after spending time with that jerk Victorius?"

"OOH, no," said Brutus. "He was AWESOME! We promised to keep in touch and everything. He HATED you, though. You really made him mad by beating him in front of thousands of people."

"He deserved it, the weasel," said Julius.

"I can't believe how much you've changed, Julius!" said Brutus. "Mom would be SO proud of you!"

Suddenly, something caught Brutus's eye. On the horizon he spotted a chariot coming over the hill.

"Hey, Julius, am I crazy, or is that a giraffe on the back of that chariot?"

"RUFUS!" cried Julius. "And wait, that's Lucia holding the reins!"

Julius dashed out and waved frantically at the chariot. "LUCIA! WE'RE HERE!"

"AMAZING!" cried Julius. "Where did you get the chariot?"

"These guys lent it to me!" said Lucia.

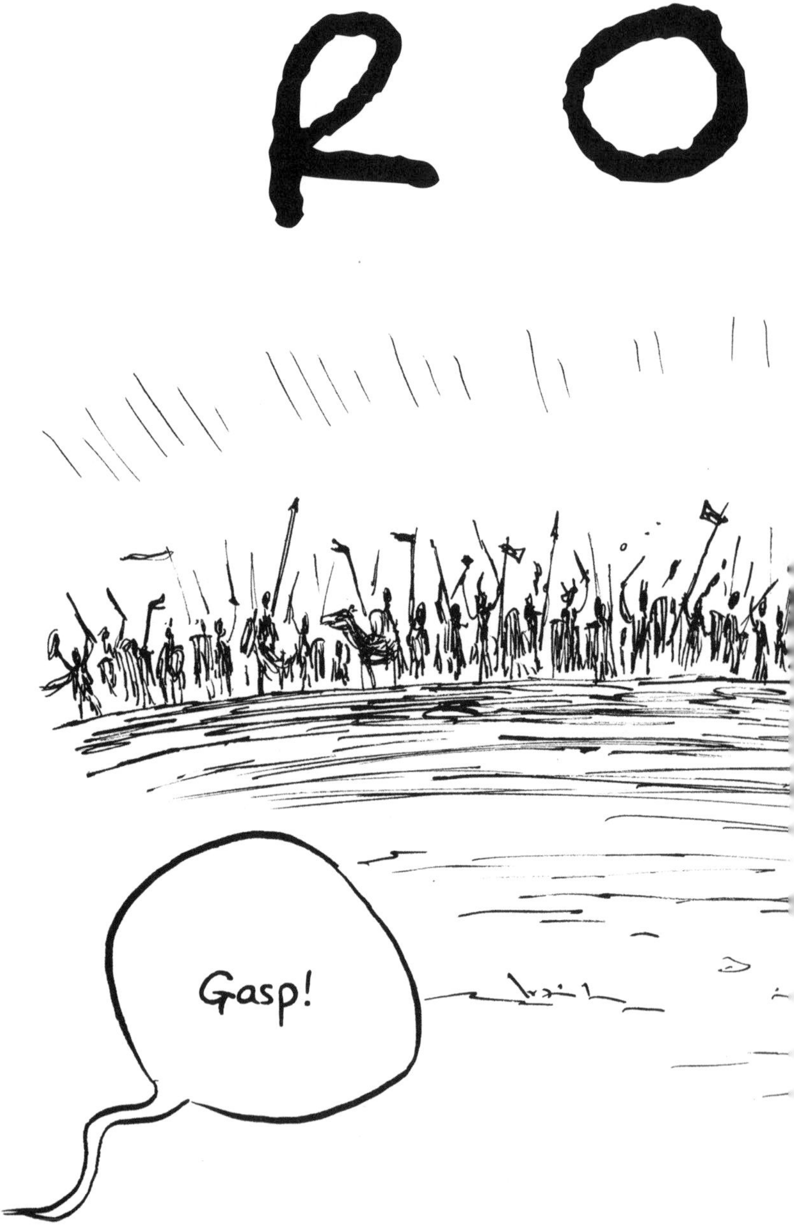

RO
Gasp!

"Pericles, Berta, and Douglas followed us all the way up to the wall, gathering warriors as they went!"

"LEAD THEM?" Julius balked. "I didn't say I'd LEAD them! I thought we'd just *work* together!"

A great chorus of swords thumping against wooden shields reverberated across the valley.

"Try telling THEM that!" Lucia chuckled.

Another chariot raced over, this one carrying Cornelius, Milus, Felix, and Pliny.

"Sounds like you've made a name for yourself HERE, too, Zebra!" Pliny laughed.

CHAPTER TWENTY-TWO

BROTHERS IN ARMS

Julius and the army of Britons approached the Roman fort.

"How many of us are there?" asked Julius.

"About two thousand," replied Lucia.

"EXCELLENT! There's only a hundred of them. This will be easy."

Hadrian stood on the fort battlements.

Lay down your arms, Zebra, and I will spare you and your friends!

"Did someone say something?" Julius asked Brutus. "I couldn't quite hear over the ROAR of my ENORMOUS ARMY." He thrust his hoof in the air and the horde of Britons charged against the fort.

The wooden gates crashed open like rotten firewood as the barbarians poured into the courtyard.

"They're running away like big chickens!" cried Brutus as every last Roman soldier ran for his life.

"Victory is OURS!" yelled Julius.

In the distance, Julius spotted Hadrian and Septimus speeding off in the emperor's golden chariot.

Julius plopped to the ground, exhausted. "They'll be back, and in greater numbers," he wheezed.

"Aye," rasped a familiar voice. "And we'll be *waiting* for them."

"DOUGLAS!" cried Julius, leaping up. He grabbed his former opponent by the hoof. "Thank you for trusting me!"

"You've given us hope, Zebra. Let's see if we can't kick these cockroaches out FOREVER!"

Julius turned to his friends. "And we're FREE! We're ACTUALLY FREE!"

We can FINALLY go home.

"But what about the other animal gladiators?" said Brutus.

"What do you mean?" asked Julius.

"Hadrian is training DOZENS of captured animals from all around the empire. Maybe we should set them free, too."

Julius looked at his brother. "What, you mean we should take on ROME ITSELF?"

"Maybe." Brutus grinned. "Or you could go back to that stinky lake and drink the stinky water. It's up to YOU!"

🌿EPILOGUE🌿

At Ludus Magnus, Rome's biggest gladiator school and home to the city's gladiator champions, the past few months had seen many changes—most not welcome to the veteran fighters.

Julius Zebra's success had prompted Hadrian to demand MORE bestial gladiators, of all shapes and sizes. The more animal gladiators on show, the happier his citizens were, and the happier his citizens were, the happier Hadrian was, too.

Except that not *all* the animals captured and put up for training were *happy* to become gladiators.

In fact, one particular recruit was proving to be extremely difficult to handle.

"It's no good, Victorius," said the bumbling

dungeon master. "No matter what I do, I can't keep her quiet!"

Victorius threw down his scroll. "DO I HAVE TO DO EVERYTHING MYSELF?" He stormed down to the school arena, where his disobedient pupil was chained to a training pole.

"By Jupiter's beard, Zebra, what will it take for you to BEHAVE yourself?"

"You will free me from these chains and take me to my SONS," demanded the zebra.

Or you will feel the sharp end of my HOOF!

TO BE CONTINUED . . .

ROMAN NUMERALS

Hello, readers! Julius has asked me and Felix to help explain the strange page numbers used throughout this book.

Instead of page numbers like 1, 2, and 3, you'll find I, V, X, and various other letters, which are Roman numerals — just like the Romans used for counting!

Even an idiot like me can understand them. Hooray!

Here are the seven letters that represent all the Roman numerals.

I = 1
V = 5
X = 10
L = 50
C = 100
D = 500
M = 1000

Thankfully, you won't find the last two. This book is big enough as it is!

Mostly, you simply add Roman numerals together to make different numbers:
II (1 + 1) = 2
VIII (5+1+1+1) = 8
CLI (100 + 50 + 1) = 151

That seems easy enough! I'm off to collect some rocks.

WAIT! We're not finished! You don't ALWAYS add Roman numerals!

Oh?

Sometimes you subtract. For instance, 3 is written as III, but 4 is not IIII.

But hold on, how do you write 4, then?

My brain hurts!

When a smaller numeral comes before a larger numeral, take away the value of the smaller numeral from the bigger one.

So 4 is IV?

Yes! And 9 is IX, and 40 is XL, and 90 is XC.

To summarize: Always read Roman numerals from left to right. If a larger numeral comes before a smaller or equal numeral, add them. But if a smaller numeral comes before a larger numeral, subtract the smaller number from the bigger one before moving on to the next letter in the row.

If there is a next letter, of course!

Here are some to help you along!

1 I	10 X	50 L
2 II	11 XI	60 LX
3 III	12 XII	70 LXX
4 IV	13 XIII	80 LXXX
5 V	14 XIV	90 XC
6 VI	15 XV	100 C
7 VII	20 XX	200 CC
8 VIII	30 XXX	
9 IX	40 XL	

❦FURTHER INFORMATION❦
WHAT THE ROMANS BROUGHT TO BRITAIN

ADVERTISING

We are bombarded by advertising at every turn these days, and life wasn't so different in Roman Britain. The Romans would stick up posters for political messages, social events, and, of course, sports events. No doubt Julius had his beautiful face drawn on such a poster!

APPLES AND PEARS

Often used by the Romans to sweeten recipes. Today, Brits tend to enjoy them in pies, crisps, and crumbles.

BATHS

Washing and gossiping were two of Rome's favorite things, which is why their baths were so popular. Widely introduced throughout Britain, the bath was such a hit that they even named a city after it! Toilets were just as popular with Romans, so I think we got off lightly there.

CALENDAR

Romans loved their calendars, and our current Gregorian calendar is a direct descendant of the old Roman calendar and Julius Caesar's Julian calendar. They gave us most of our months, including September (from the Latin *septem,* meaning seven), October (from the Latin *octo,* meaning eight), November (from the Latin *novem,* meaning nine), and December (from the Latin *decem,* meaning ten). We've added a couple of months to our calendar since, so those names don't make much sense now!

CARROTS

Originally came in red, black, yellow, and white, as well as the familiar orange. Romans found them useful for medicine and for feeding all the rabbits that had recently turned up. (*See* Rabbits)

CATS

Brought over as mascots by the Roman Army, domestic cats were also revered as gods of liberty. This meant they could come and go as they pleased, a privilege unchanged for the last two thousand years.

CEMENT

Being great engineers, the Romans used copious amounts of cement to construct their statues and buildings, plenty of which survive today. Workers even added volcanic ash to the mixture, which, when left in water, would set as hard as rock. Whether Roman construction workers were also behind the origin of "plumber's crack" is not so clear.

CENTRAL HEATING

Villas and baths were kept warm and cozy for chilly Romans by the circulation of warm air pumped up through holes in the floor and walls via a furnace tended by slaves. The warm air vents were also greatly appreciated by lazy cats.

FLUSHING TOILETS

Thanks to their great ingenuity and love of cleanliness, Romans introduced continuously flowing water to their latrines. Toilets were communal, so you could sit and merrily chat with your buddies as you did your business.

LANGUAGE

The Roman language, Latin, still permeates modern English to this day. Initially adopted by the aristocracy for official documents, people of all classes now use Latin phrases *ad infinitum*. (See what I did there?)

LAW AND ORDER

The Romans introduced the world's first organized police force, run much like an army, throughout their empire.

PAVED STREETS

The Romans built the first towns in Britain, introducing rigid grid networks of paved streets running between big stone buildings. The Britons had never seen anything quite like it!

PEAS

Originally brought over by the Romans from the Middle East, peas are now an important staple of the British Sunday roast. Not so great on toast (believe me, I've tried).

RABBITS

Rabbits were first domesticated by the Romans, who bred them for their meat, fur, and wool. And also because they were cute, with adorable little faces. Probably.

STINGING NETTLES

Used by Romans for treating sore muscles and also for keeping legs warm by slapping them against the skin. Nowadays stinging nettle soup is sold in fancy supermarkets in the spring.

STRAIGHT ROADS

When the Romans got to Britain, muddy, twisty-turny roads were OUT; straight stone roads were IN — all ten thousand miles of them. The Romans made their roads straight so that their marching army could invade your rebellious village even more quickly. Hooray!

TURNIPS

Widely used by Romans as food for livestock during the cold winter months. Wow, eating turnips on a cold, wet day, standing in a muddy field: sheep and cows always knew how to have a good time.

WINE

Water was very unsafe to drink two thousand years ago, so Romans drank wine instead. Wine was so popular with the Romans that they drank 25 million gallons (100 million liters) a year in the city of Rome alone! In Britain everyone drank cheap beer, but the Romans hated the stuff, so they stuck to their wine.

FELIX'S AWESOME ROCK COLLECTION

Green and sparkly

Rock with grass
growing out of it

Coughed up by a duck

Piece of the Pyramid of Giza

Almost like bacon

Nose fallen off a statue

Looks like the Moon

Lucky stone
(My second one; lost
the first one.)

Looks a bit like Julius

Found under my bed

Street cobblestone

Reminds me of home

Identical stones

Dropped from my ear

Amber with fly inside

Stone from Londinium river

From the race track at
the Circus Maximus

Volcanic sponge

Actually floats

Emperor Nero's favorite rock
(replica)

Fell off the Colosseum

Smallest stone in the world

Old stone tooth

From Hadrian's garden